CONTENTS

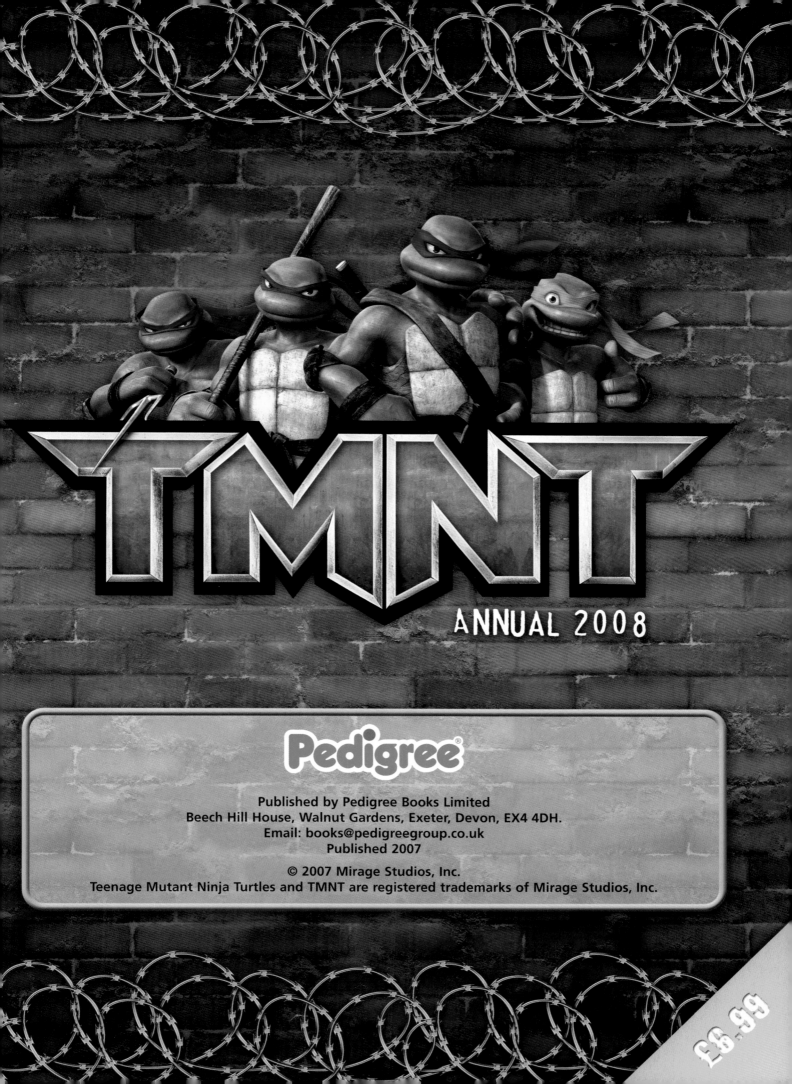

TMNT

ANNUAL 2008

Pedigree®

Published by Pedigree Books Limited
Beech Hill House, Walnut Gardens, Exeter, Devon, EX4 4DH.
Email: books@pedigreegroup.co.uk
Published 2007

£6.99

TMNT

GOOD GUYS

LEONARDO

Leo is the unofficial leader of the four Teenage Mutant Ninja Turtles brothers and so dedicated to his ninjitsu training that the other turtles jokingly refer to him as "Splinter Junior." Although he likes to take the lead and come up with battle strategies, Leo is also a team player and will listen to suggestions that are the best for the group. Leonardo's weapons of choice are the twin katana blades. Leo has just undertaken a year-long, around-the-world training mission in order to take his ninja skills to the next level.

SPLINTER

RAPHAEL

Master Splinter is the Turtles' sensei -their teacher- who has taught them their ninjitsu skills and bushido (way of the warrior) philosophy. He is the sewer rat who mutated alongside the baby turtles, rescued them and brought them up as though they were his own children, giving them the love and care they needed as they were growing up. Before mutating, Splinter was once the pet rat of a ninja master, Hamato Yoshi. It was through watching and mimicking Yoshi's martial arts moves that Splinter learned ninjitsu.

Brash, restless, opinionated, stubborn and temperamental, Raphael is nearly the very opposite of his brother Leonardo in almost every regard (which is why the sparks often fly between the two brothers). Raphael loves the physical aspects of ninjitsu -he loves to fight!- and trains with single-minded intensity. The hot-headed Raphael often likes to fight first and ask questions later. His flashing twin steel sais and his hair-trigger temper make Raphael a fearsome and fearless warrior.

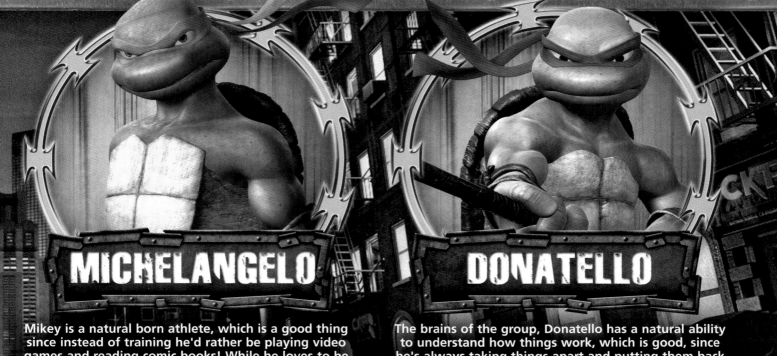

MICHELANGELO

DONATELLO

Mikey is a natural born athlete, which is a good thing since instead of training he'd rather be playing video games and reading comic books! While he loves to be the centre of attention, Mikey's sense of humour and easy-going nature make him the group's natural peacemaker. He's also a pop culture sponge who can never cram enough television, DVDs, CDs, videogames, comic books and magazines into the day! Splinter selected the whirling nunchakus as the weapon best suited to this turtle's buoyant spirit. He earns extra money by dressing up as Cowabung Carl and performing for children's birthday parties.

The brains of the group, Donatello has a natural ability to understand how things work, which is good, since he's always taking things apart and putting them back together - correctly! Donnie is quite the inventor as well, having either invented or customized the Turtles' Shell Cells, Night-vision Binoculars, Sewer Jacuzzi, and more computers than he can remember! He can build high-speed vehicles and turtlized accessories out of little more than scraps and trash salvaged from a junk yard. Because Donatello is stout of heart, Splinter gave his the stout bo staff as his signature weapon.

CASEY JONES

APRIL O'NEIL

You think Raphael has a temper? Well, Casey Jones makes Raphael look absolute mellow! Which may explain why the two have become the best of buddies! Casey is a vigilante who stalks the mean streets of New York looking for trouble… and when he finds it the bad guys better beware because Casey is out to right wrongs and doesn't mind busting a few bad guy heads in the process! With his trademark hockey mask and golf bag full of sports equipment, Casey is one tough hombre! Still, this hot-head has a soft sport for the love of his life, April O'Neil.

Just as smart and scientifically savvy as Donatello, April is a trained scientist and computer engineer. Lately she has taken up training with Leonardo, and is beginning to master the katana sword. April also runs her own business -Second Time Around- an antiques and vintage clothing store. About a year ago she started working for the mysterious multi-millionaire, Max Winters, often traveling the globe in search of precious ancient goods for his growing collection of oddities.

TMNT BAD GUYS

Since the death of the Shredder, leadership of the clan of criminal ninja known as the Foot, has fallen to his adopted daughter, Karai. Little is known of Karai, although her skills with the katana sword rival those of Leo.

KARAI

The Foot is a global criminal organization based in New York City whose history, traditions and practices are based on the ways of ninjitsu… but twisted towards evil ends. Now led by Karai, the Foot is made up of many divisions, including the Foot Soldier (ninja), Elite Guard, Technicians, Mystics, and Geneticists.

THE FOOT

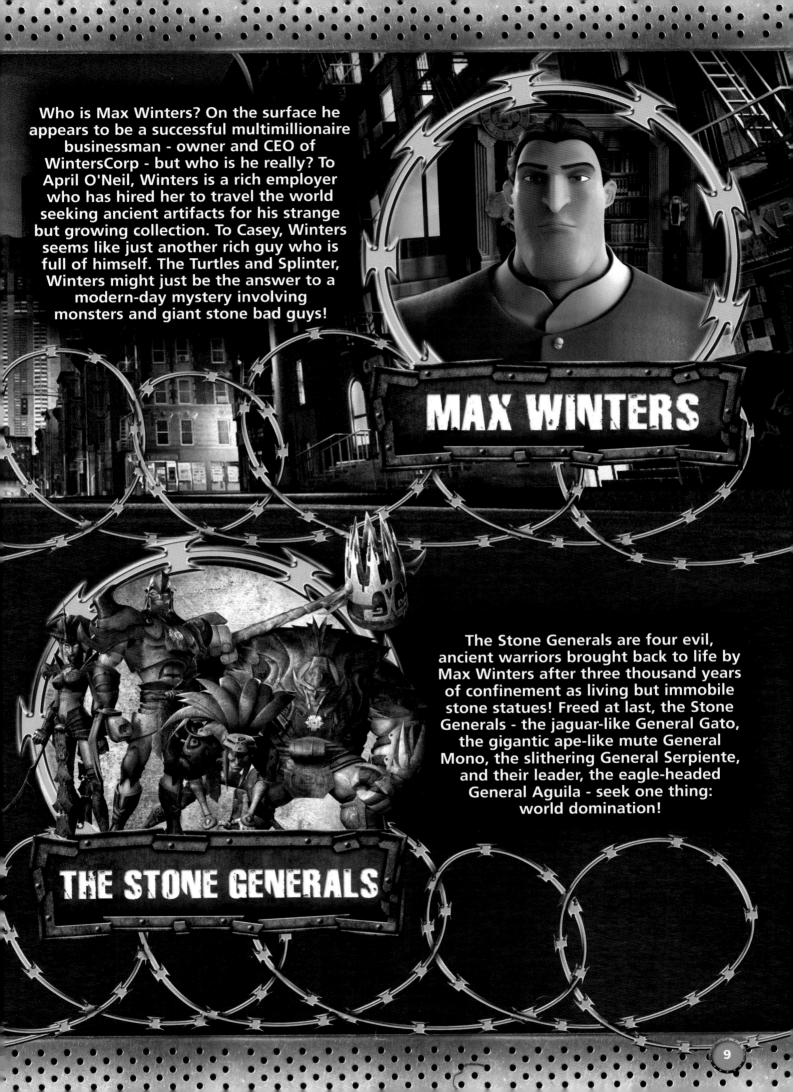

Who is Max Winters? On the surface he appears to be a successful multimillionaire businessman - owner and CEO of WintersCorp - but who is he really? To April O'Neil, Winters is a rich employer who has hired her to travel the world seeking ancient artifacts for his strange but growing collection. To Casey, Winters seems like just another rich guy who is full of himself. The Turtles and Splinter, Winters might just be the answer to a modern-day mystery involving monsters and giant stone bad guys!

MAX WINTERS

The Stone Generals are four evil, ancient warriors brought back to life by Max Winters after three thousand years of confinement as living but immobile stone statues! Freed at last, the Stone Generals - the jaguar-like General Gato, the gigantic ape-like mute General Mono, the slithering General Serpiente, and their leader, the eagle-headed General Aguila - seek one thing: world domination!

THE STONE GENERALS

TMNT
THE STORY

Deep in the rainforests of **Central America...**

Ha! Ha! Ha! Nothing like robbing from the poor and giving to the rich!

Look! Up ahead - **the ghost of the jungle!**

...a gang of criminals drives away after robbing the poor inhabitants of a remote village.

Who are you? Show yourself.

Boo.

I am not afraid of some myth! I'm not afraid of some ghost!

You should be.

Leonardo defeats the criminal with two swift strokes of his katana blades.

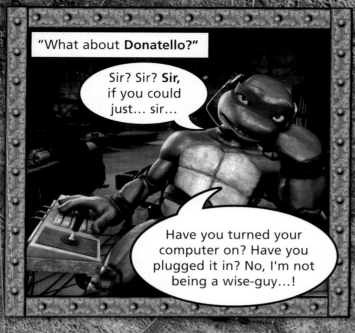

"What about **Donatello?**"

Sir? Sir? **Sir,** if you could just... sir...

Have you turned your computer on? Have you plugged it in? No, I'm not being a wise-guy...!

"But Donnie's a genius. Why'd he take a job like that?

What? Oh. Uh, sorry, **ma'am.**

"And who's keeping an eye on **Michelangelo?**"

"No one. Mikey's gotten into the, um... entertainment business."

Happy birthday...

...from **Cowabunga Carl!**

Take it easy, little dudes!

Ow! Stop it! No more sugar for you!

"Your family needs you, Leo. Your brothers have lost their way."

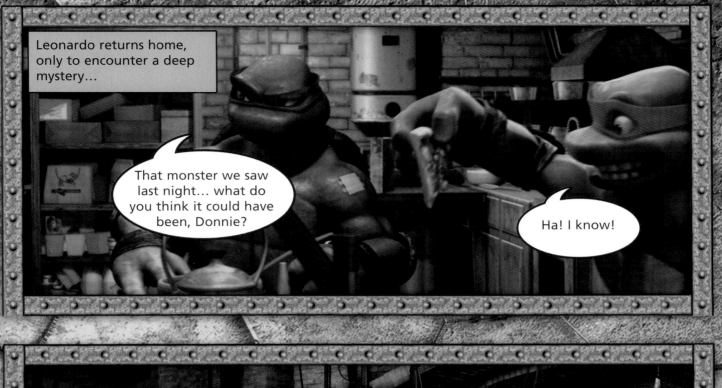

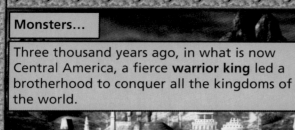

Monsters…

Three thousand years ago, in what is now Central America, a fierce **warrior king** led a brotherhood to conquer all the kingdoms of the world.

Nothing could stand in their way.

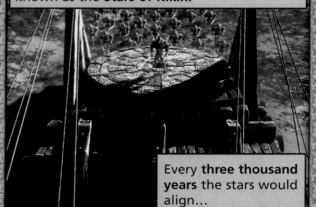

In his quest for power and immortality, the great warrior learned of a celestial body known as the **Stars of Kikin.**

Every **three thousand years** the stars would align…

…opening a portal to unknown power and thirteen cursed **monsters.**

The warrior received immortality… but at a price.

Aaaarrrgh!

He was condemned to eternally walk the earth with the weight of his mistake and its lonely consequences forever on his shoulders.

His four generals…

…were turned to living stone, frozen alive forever.

New York. Three thousand years later

The skyscraper headquarters of the **Winters Corporation**…

…and the mysterious millionaire **Max Winters**.

It has taken me countless years…

…but I have finally brought together all four **Stone Generals** and restored them to life.

Now I need you and your funky bunch to help me round up thirteen strange visitors to our city.

No one refers to the **Foot Clan** with such disrespect! No one!

No?

Well, I just did.

Grrrrrr.

Good thing I like you, **Karai.** I'll overlook your sticking that popsicle in my face…

…and let you **live.**

Now… get to work.

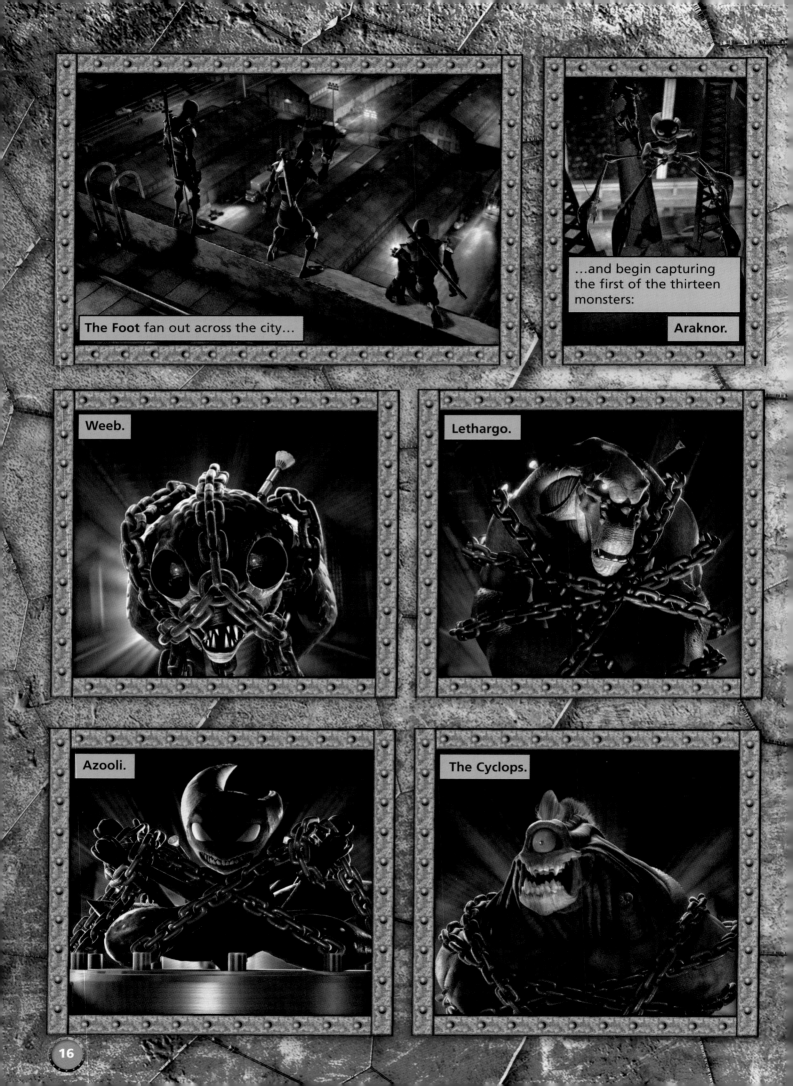

The Foot fan out across the city…

…and begin capturing the first of the thirteen monsters:

Araknor.

Weeb.

Lethargo.

Azooli.

The Cyclops.

CROSSWORD PUZZLE

How well do you know the TMNT?
See if you can figure out the proper answer from the clues below.

ACROSS
4. Raphael's Weapon
5. Wears a Hockey Mask
6. Leonardo's Weapon
7. Went Around the World to Train
9. Works in Computer Support

DOWN
1. Nightwatcher's Secret Identity
2. Cowabunga Carl's Secret Identity
3. Raised the Turtles
8. Donatello's Weapon
10. Michelangelo's Weapon

WHAT'S DIFFERENT?

Look closely at the four pictures of Michelangelo below.
Can you tell what's different in each picture?

A

B

C

D

"…Raphael."

My built-in police scanner says there's been a new monster sighting…

"…right down there, in that diner!"

Look at you. Ain't you the cutest little monster?

Urm?

SNARRRL! BLEHH! HISSSS!

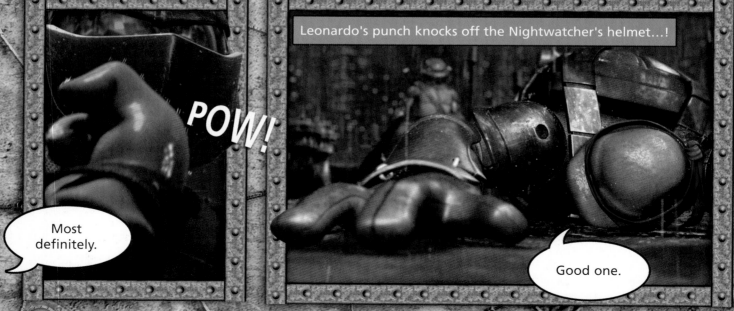

WHO AM I?

Can you identify the four TMNT and their friends from their shadows below? Write their names in the boxes below each picture. Answers are at the bottom of the page.

A

B

C

D

E

F

DESIGN A TURTLE ROBOT

Donatello has been working hard in his lab to create a robotic turtle to help the TMNT in their fight for good. But he needs your help to finish the design. In the space below, draw the Turtle Robot's weapons. Be sure to color in his mask and belt. At the bottom of your picture, write the Turtle Robot's name. (It can be an Italian artist's name, or something else - whatever you want!)

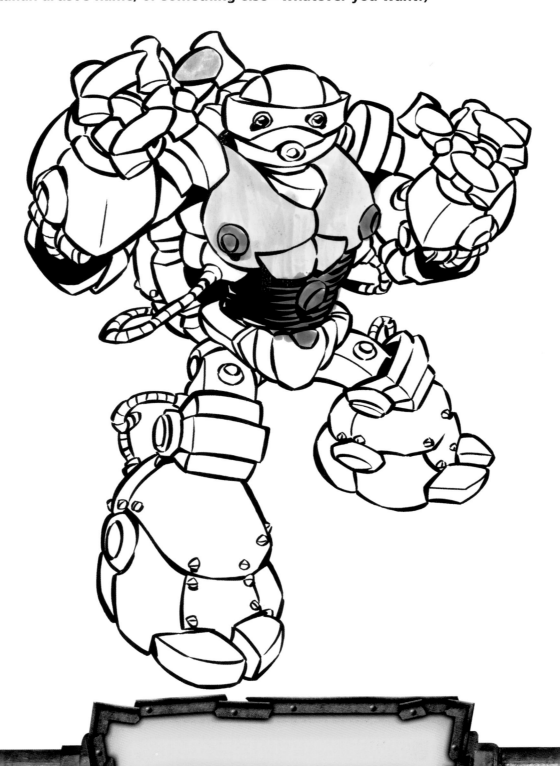

Across the city, events begin to converge…

…at the headquarters of the Winters Corporation.

In the skies above, a hurricane-like storm begins to gather its strength…

…while below, Karai prepares to protect the corporate grounds…

Come to me, my ninja.

…aided by hundreds of Foot Ninja.

Prepare yourselves for battle.

Time to storm the castle!

True. But how do we keep the Foot **out?**

We're **in!**

You boys leave it to **me.**

Casey triggers an alarm, and the security gates slide shut.

Too cool!

Can't touch me!

Donatello manages to unlock the cell...

USE YOUR COLOURING PENS TO COLOUR THIS PICTURE OF THE SEWERDWELLING HEROES.

It's **Max Winters!**

Bogus.

Is he... dead?

Must be. No one coulda survived falling down all that way...

...right?

Ur... wrong.

Great oogly-moogly!

He... he's alive?!

The curse of immortality. There is no escape, no release...

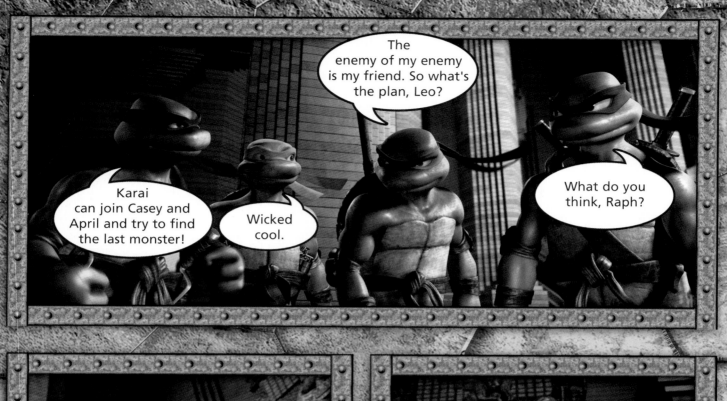

WORD SEARCH

The TMNT are skilled in the ancient martial art ninjitsu. Look below to find words relating to ninjas. They can appear forward, backward, up, down, or diagonally.

```
M P I N V I S I B L E L
E S A S J V N A R A G D
D X W G H A W M V R E B
I Y R O P A N C I E N T
T R Z A R S D D E I L S
A E J F L D X O D M V H
T T C D M U S F W O S O
I S N E K I R U H S J B
O A H C N T Y L L P F O
N M A B Q S A S D Y D S
S R E K C A R C E R I F
```

MEDITATION	☐	INVISIBLE	☐	SHOBO	☐
SHADOWS	☐	SWORDS	☐	MASTER	☐
ANCIENT	☐	SPY	☐	DOJO	☐
SHURIKEN	☐	FIRECRACKERS	☐	JAPAN	☐

CASEY CUT OUT

Casey Jones is going out for a night on patrol. Help him get ready by cutting out the pictures of Casey and his weapons. With tape, stick the weapons in Casey's hands, and put his mask on.

Make sure you get help when using the scissors.

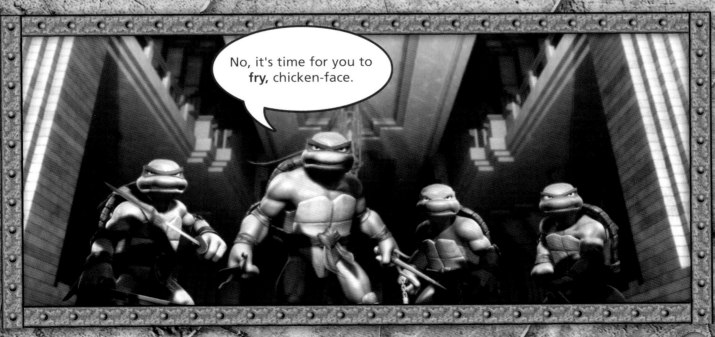

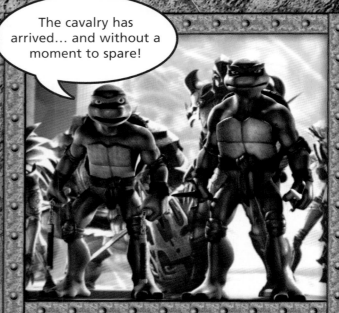

Casey.

Thank you, April, Chester.

I think you owe your thanks to more than just we two, Max...

Of course. I should thank you all... and then bid you farewell.

What, you got a bus to catch or something?

Hush, Michelangelo.

Nasty.

What is happening to you, Mister Winters?

With the monsters returned to their homeworld, the curse has been lifted... and my immortality comes to an end.

Farewell, my friends...

...farewell!

FZZZT!

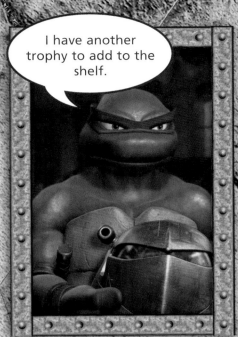

The TMNT are named after the great artists of the Renaissance. Read the clues, and see if you can identify which artists our heroes were named after. Answers below.

1
- Painted the *Mona Lisa*
- Designed flying machines
- A popular book and movie named for him

I AM

2
- Painted the ceiling of a famous cathedral
- Well known sculptor
- Worked as an architect

I AM

3
- Made his statues look deeper than they were
- Known for sculpting soldiers
- Often used wood for his sculptures

I AM

4
- Painted many battle scenes
- Liked to paint portraits of important people
- Most famous painting is *School of Athens*

I AM

MAZE

Leonardo is searching for the mysterious Nightwatcher somewhere in New York City. Help Leo find the Nightwatcher by guiding him through the maze below

ANSWERS

Page 19
What's Different?

A

B

C

D

R A P H A E L

S A I

M I C H E L A N G E L

C A S E Y

S P L I N T E R

K A T A N A

L E O N A R D O

B O S T A F F

D O N A T E L L O

N U N C H A K U

Page 18
Crossword
Puzzle